Praise for Storyshares

"One of the brightest innovators and game-changers in the education industry."
— Forbes

"Your success in applying research-validated practices to promote literacy serves as a valuable model for other organizations seeking to create evidence-based literacy programs."
— Library of Congress

"We need powerful social and educational innovation, and Storyshares is breaking new ground. The organization addresses critical problems facing our students and teachers. I am excited about the strategies it brings to the collective work of making sure every student has an equal chance in life."
— Teach For America

"It's the perfect idea. There's really nothing like this. I mean, wow, this will be a wonderful experience for young people."
— Andrea Davis Pinkney, Executive Director, Scholastic

"Reading for meaning opens opportunities for a lifetime of learning. Providing emerging readers with engaging texts that are designed to offer both challenges and support for each individual will improve their lives for years to come. Storyshares is a wonderful start."
— David Rose, Co-founder of CAST & UDL

Snap

Storyshares presents

Published by Storyshares, LLC
Inspiring reading with a new kind of book.

Storyshares
Storyshares, LLC
24 N. Bryn Mawr Avenue #340
Bryn Mawr, Pennsylvania 19010-3304
www.storyshares.org

Interest Level: High School
Grade Level Equivalent: 3

ISBN 9798885978118
Book design by Saskia Globig

Snap

Sophene Avedissian

Storyshares

Contents

ONE

The City That Never Sleeps

The streets are lifeless, empty, and dark.

The crowd of the usual tourists is gone. The traffic is flowing smoothly, like a river, with only a few cars on the road. The whole city is covered by black, silky darkness.

The only thing that's active is light.

Light is everywhere. It is shining in office buildings that are at least seven hundred feet tall. It's in crowded apartments, restaurants, and vehicles.

I am in the city that never sleeps. The city that has a beautiful skyline.

There are only a few visible stars in the sky. The lights are too bright and overpowering. It is magical. It's nothing like what I am used to.

It's nothing like Smallview.

It is quiet. The only sounds I can hear are cars driving over puddles of water. Splash. Splash. Splash.

I make the same sounds with every step I take. I splash my mustard-yellow rubber boots in the dark pools of water.

The rain keeps drizzling. I notice the water droplets collected on the hood of my raincoat, like ants in cracks of concrete.

The strong smell of gasoline from the cars floats to my nose, along with the smell of food from the busy restaurants.

An Italian restaurant, a bakery filled with all kinds of desserts, and a cart full of Mexican food are next to each other. Each of them is filled with dozens and dozens of people. They're packed in together like a playoff game at Yankee Stadium.

Standing on my tiptoes, I read the name of a small pastry shop. It is the same size as a closet.

"Minnie's Treats," I whisper to myself.

A young couple chats over a piece of custard pie and coffee. The tip of the woman's fork is coated with her glossy red lipstick.

Next to them sits an old lady with curled, cream-colored hair. She has a stunning rose quartz ring on her finger.

Sitting in front of the window is a middle-aged man. He is so attached to his phone that he has not even looked at the cup of tea that sits on his table. The hot Earl Grey tea makes steam float out of the brown mug.

The pastel colors of the pastry shop stand out on the street. Maybe this street is not so lifeless, after all.

I keep walking down the street. I run my frozen, numb fingers through my damp hair.

There are two girls behind me. They're about my age. One of them is wearing an outfit like mine: black leggings, yellow boots, and a raincoat. The other girl wears a long-sleeved beige dress with wool tights and chunky, black ankle boots.

Each whisper between them is followed by laughter. They soon pass by me. One of the girls quickly looks back at me. She gives me a small, gentle smile. I smile back.

I do not miss Smallview.

The mood here is like no other. I am complete-ly happy. For once in a long time, I feel free.

Smallview makes me feel like a mummy wrapped in linen cloth. The town masks parts of me, hiding who I truly am. Smallview covers me with a thick, bulky cast. But here, the cast is finally being taken off.

Now, I have myself back. I am no longer held back.

13

I pass by different bars, clubs, coffee shops, and restaurants, but I am not drawn to any of them. Walking on the street and being able to watch everything is perfect. In fact, it is the closest thing to perfect I have ever experienced.

With each step toward the end of the street, I hear my breathing. The soft, low breaths soon become heavy as I start walking faster.

It is starting to rain harder. The small droplets of water on my raincoat have turned into puddles. Tucking my hands into the pockets of my raincoat, I start running. The top of my head gets showered with water like grass when sprinklers are turned on.

The rain starts pouring down. The drops from the sky hit even harder. The same sound is repeated, like the thumping of a heartbeat.

The droplets hit the roofs of cars. Thump. Thump. Thump.

The sky is covering the city in rain.

Around the corner is a cute coffeehouse. It has yellow walls and a coffee mug rack that covers most of the back wall. The paint is faded. I can tell right away that this shop has been here much longer than me.

There is no one else there except one woman. She is standing behind the counter, texting someone on her phone. I take one more step toward the table by the window.

The woman quickly raises her head. Her ice-cold, blue eyes look right into my hazelnut-brown ones. Her hawk eyes do not match her kind, welcoming attitude.

"Hey there, honey. Is there anything I can get for you?" she asks.

"Yes, please. I'll have a large hot coffee," I answer.

"Of course! I'll get it right to you, but for now, please sit down at a table," she says.

I nod and walk toward the table I had my eye on earlier. Taking a seat and crossing my legs, I wait for my coffee.

The sweet woman brings me my coffee in seconds.

She pulls her blonde hair behind her ears. "Would you like any sugar or cream?" she asks

"No, thank you. I like it black," I answer.

As I pick up the mug, I look straight at the glass window in front of me. I stare at the reflection of myself. I study my posture. I like this new person I see in the glass. I like everything about her.

Finally, I feel at home.

Snap.

It all goes dark. Black.

Everything is gone. The woman, the table, the chairs, my coffee, my reflection.

I open my eyes to a room with a furry, turquoise rug and a white desk with a stack of books. There are posters of my favorite cities on the walls: New York, Paris, Las Vegas, Malibu, and New Orleans. It is my room. My room in Smallview.

Frustration fills me. Burying my head under the covers of my bed, I wait for my alarm to go off.

I hoped it would be hours. It was only a few seconds.

Beep. Beep. Beep.

TWO

The City of Light

People always tell me I look exactly like my mom, Diana.

We both have short, light brown hair. It matches the color of our almond-shaped eyes. We both have a button nose and full, light pink lips.

But I want the comparison to stop there. She is stuck, trapped. I never want to be in that position.

Before leaving my room, I take one more look around. I look at the posters. I close my eyes, imagining that I am in one of those magical cities.

"All right, let's do this," I mumble to myself.

After slipping into my striped grey-and-white sneakers, I walk downstairs. I find my dad eating breakfast. On his plate are two scrambled eggs, a piece of toast, and a few slices of bacon.

He does not even notice I'm there.

"Hey, Dad. Where's Mom?" I ask.

He keeps looking at his phone.

He answers in an impatient tone, "I think she's with Celeste."

"Okay, thanks. I have to go," I say.

Standing still like a statue, I wait for a goodbye. A few seconds go by. Dad has not said anything. Finally, after waiting a bit more, I give up.

I walk quickly to the kitchen counter to grab a few cookies from the jar. The cookie jar is the last of my relationship with Dad. Ever since I was a toddler, he has filled it with cookies.

Dad put in oatmeal raisin cookies today. It is a change from the chocolate chip I usually find.

I leave the house with breakfast to go: a strawberry-flavored yogurt cup, a couple of cookies, and a chocolate croissant that Celeste made a couple of days ago.

The croissant tastes slightly stale. But the flavor of butter with dark chocolate melts in my mouth like snow on fire.

A voice nearby catches my attention.

"Leila! Leila, come here!"

I turn around to see Celeste wearing hot pink gardening gloves. She has a black trowel in her right hand. Her long, blonde hair looks nice with her light blue sweater.

There is a mound of dirt next to a row of colorful roses. It looks like a groundhog spent all night digging. The grass is a stunning green, the color of parsley.

Looking to the side, I stare at my house's lawn. The grass is dying. Light green and yellow patches cover the whole lawn. The blades of grass are thin, frayed, and torn. It's the opposite of Celeste's.

Every morning, Mom has coffee and chats with Celeste while she gardens. The garden is Celeste's escape, her getaway.

Mom is sitting in a rocking chair on the patio. With her shoulders rolled back and posture straight, she keeps laughing and talking. She hasn't noticed me.

"Uh, Diana. Look who's here," Celeste says. She points her finger at me.

"Leila, good! Do you want to come sit?" Mom asks.

"No, thanks. I have to get to school early for a group project," I answer.

"Okay, well, I'll see you later," Mom says.

I smile and nod. "Sounds good. Bye, Mom," I say.

Smallview High School is a few blocks away. It's right next to Dad's restaurant, The Bun Corner.

As I walk toward the end of the street, I hear the sweet sounds of Mom's giggles. She is the happiest I have ever seen her. She always is, with Celeste.

It is only with Celeste that she sits tall and keeps her head up. It is only with Celeste that she feels real and human. Inside the house, she shrivels like she is a piece of crumpled paper about to be thrown away in a trashcan.

Unfortunately, this break from reality is short. Soon, regret will begin eating away at her again, like termites in wood.

I wish this escape was permanent. I wish a lot of things could change.

Dad is not any better than Mom. To Smallview, he is "the hot dog king." He owns the most popular and successful restaurant in the whole town. I only wish he was the same person at home.

I breathe deeply in and out. I drop my hands to my sides. I close my eyes. My feet keep moving, but my body feels like it is floating on cool, refreshing water.

Fluttering my eyes open, I see everything I want to see. I am in a place where I want to be. The sound of cars driving and the footsteps of tourists and locals make a song. It's like the songs played in the Palais Garnier Opera House.

Leaves twirl on the street like ballerinas in

a dance performance. Their apricot-orange and butterscotch-yellow colors stand out on the charcoal-black ground. With each step I take, the street brightens more and more.

My slow walking turns into a jog. Finally, I see it. I am captured by its golden-yellow color. The Eiffel Tower looks like it is covered in sparkles and glitter. The shining beacon is a powerful nightlight for the entire city.

I do not blink for what seems like a lifetime. I can't take my eyes off of the tower. It does not look like what I have seen in pictures. Standing in front of it, I get to admire every detail.

Trying to take in all one thousand feet of it, I raise my head. I wish I could stand at the very top. I would see everything: the restaurants, shops, and the tiny, black dots that are people. The slight breeze would wrap around my body, the chill blowing over me.

I look down. The picture of looking over the entire city from the tip of the tower is being erased from my mind.

Snap.

It all goes dark. Black.

My head is still facing down, but the glow from the tower has disappeared. Now, "Smallview High School" are the words I see. They're written on the concrete in red and blue letters along with our mascot, an eagle.

A crowd of people walks through the glass doors with silver handles. I stand still, not moving. I notice the familiar smell of flowery perfume. Right away, I know Maya is nearby.

I look in the opposite direction, avoiding any eye contact. I cannot face her. I cannot face this school.

As I take a couple of steps forward, I think of the posters in my room. Knowing they will be in my room when I go back home is calming.

In a few hours, I will be able to close my eyes and go into a different world. It is the push I need to get through the day ahead of me.

Ring. Ring. Ring.

THREE

The City of
Second Chances

In Smallview, most people are wrapped in their cozy comforters. They're ready to close their eyes and doze off by 9:00 pm.

It is the complete opposite here.

Neon lights and signs of all colors make the streets feel like a nightclub. Their orange-red, green, and pink colors make a disco ball for everyone to dance under.

Walking through this city is the same as walking on the red carpet. You feel like you are the most important person in the world. Here, there is a spotlight on me. It is a nice feeling, one I have never experienced before.

People coming out of casinos are dressed formally. Most women wear long evening dresses and black, shimmering high heels. The men are dressed in white shirts, black dinner jackets, bow ties, and leather shoes. They look classy, put-together, and neat.

Other people wear yellow shirts with flamingos and palm trees on them, along with athletic shorts and fisherman sandals. They look like they are getting off of an airplane in Hawaii or Florida. Like they're ready to lounge by the pool while sipping on an umbrella-topped drink.

I pass by the lines for clubs and restaurants. They are as long as the lines at clothing stores on Black Friday.

Across the street is a place called Dinner in the Clouds. Its red sign above the door is written in cursive. A couple and two women in their twenties wait outside to be let in.

After fixing my untied shoelace, I cross the street. I go to stand behind the middle-aged couple.

The wife whispers in her husband's ear. It reminds me of the telephone game I played with my friends when I was much younger.

The husband brings his wife closer to him. He puts his arm around her shoulder. He kisses her.

The woman giggles and kisses him on his

cheek. It smears her sparkling pink lipstick on him. He is too happy to not ce.

"Miss, you can come in now," an employee says.

"Thank you, sir," I say.

The restaurant has a bar and a floor for dancing. I quietly sneak to the back of the room, taking a seat at a booth.

In a few moments, a waiter comes to my table.

"Miss, is there a drink I can get you?" he asks.

"I'll have a Shirley Temple, thank you," I say.

The music sounds like the pop songs I used to listen to in elementary school. I would grab my purple hairbrush, stand on top of my bed, and start singing like I was Taylor Swift at a concert.

I deeply miss those days. Those days of inno- cence.

Soon, my drink is served. The grenadine and the Sprite have not mixed yet. The drink looks like a lava lamp.

"I put in three cherries instead of two," the wait- er says.

I laugh and smile. He does the same.

After mixing my drink, I take a small sip. The bubbles and fruity flavor burst in my mouth. I put a cherry in my mouth. The sweet and sugary taste stays in my mouth even after I swallow.

There is only one woman on the dance floor. Her dark brown hair moves with her, swaying from side to side. She does not care if everyone else is staring at her. She is just dancing. Just enjoying her life and ignoring judgment from others.

I wish I was like her.

As soon as I finish my drink, I wave goodbye to the waiter. I walk out the door and into the chilly night air.

Not having anyplace in mind, I walk aimlessly down the street. I look through the windows of stores.

There is one store named Fuller's Threads. A few items are being displayed in the window. I can see a peach-colored handbag with daisies printed all over, a straw hat with a brown bow, and a beige pair of Cuban heels. The bright green sign reads *Sorry, we're closed.*

Next to Fuller's Threads is a thrift store. Inside, it looks like a teenager's messy room. Clothes are scattered everywhere, with no sections to separate the different types of clothing.

The rest of the stores are pitch black. It is impossible to see anything.

In a few minutes, I reach the end of the street. I stop next to a bench. I decide to take a seat, since I have nowhere else to go.

I hear the electronic music from the clubs a few blocks over. I smell burgers and fries from a fast-food restaurant nearby. With my legs crossed and my head resting against the back of the bench, I look at the sky. It looks so blank and empty.

I never want to leave this spot.

Snap.

It all goes dark. Black.

The chatter of Mom and Celeste downstairs reaches my room.

"Leila! Celeste is here. Come say hello, please," Mom says.

Before I open my eyes, I take a deep breath. I try to remember that soon, I will be able to go back.

"Coming, Mom!" I answer, with a little bit of attitude.

From the smudge of dirt on Celeste's left cheek and the stains of mud on her pants, I can tell that she has been gardening for hours. Mom is wearing the same outfit she wore yesterday: a grey, long-sleeved shirt and black sweatpants.

"How are you, dear?" Celeste asks.

"A little tired, but I'm fine. How are you?" I ask.

"Well, I'm actually fantastic," Celeste says. "I spent the whole morning outside."

I have never understood why Celeste gardens all the time. Does she love having dirty hands? Is she bored?

"Are you hungry? Celeste brought turkey and Swiss cheese sandwiches," Mom says.

"Not really, but I do want a snack," I say.

I walk over to the counter, to the cookie jar.

It is empty.

I pinch myself on the skin between my thumb and index finger to stop myself from crying. The pain distracts me for a couple of moments. Soon, my eyes are covered with a shining layer of tears, but I do not blink.

I will not cry in front of Mom and Celeste. I do not have the energy to explain myself.

"Mom, do you know if Dad's here?" I ask.

"No, he's not," she says. "He's at work, as usual. But you can hang out with us. Why don't you take a seat on the couch?"

I walk over to the sofa. I sink into the cushion like I am in quicksand.

Why would Dad not fill the jar? Did he forget?

The coffee table is covered in crumpled paper. Curiously, I open one of them up. I try not to make any noise for Mom to hear.

"Smallview Times Application" is printed at the top of the page. Mom has wanted to be a journalist since she was my age, but she got pregnant with me toward the end of college. Her plan fell apart. She fell apart, too.

Since then, she has not been able to pick herself back up again.

FOUR

A Paralyzing Wave

I have never seen them so angry.

Mom's face is beet red. Her cheeks look like they are sunburned.

Dad's eyes are squinting and his lips are narrow, almost like he is biting them. He yells until his voice begins to crack.

Standing in front of them and watching them argue makes me want to cry and scream. I can't handle their argument a second longer.

I rush upstairs, run into my room, and slam the door as loud as I can. I want them to know how they are hurting me. How they are both ruining our family with every angry word they say.

To Smallview, we are the perfect family. But no one knows what happens behind the closed doors of our house.

The posters on the sky-blue walls welcome me as soon as I step into the room. They are all bright and relaxing. They're the only escape I have.

I can hear the way Mom and Dad speak to each other, how they call each other names. I take a few steps forward. I stare at the poster with a dark blue ocean. Their voices become fainter and fainter.

The satisfying feeling of walking on sand makes me feel like I am at a spa. The wet sand feels solid, but mushy. It is between my toes, tickling me.

I take a step toward the water. Just like that, my feet are clean.

The breeze almost steals my hat, but I put my hand on top of my head. The salty smell of the ocean makes every worry and negative thought vanish.

As the seagulls around me squawk, I keep walking. All I see in the distance is sand. The wind runs through my hair like a blow dryer. The ends of my hair brush against my left cheek.

After a few minutes, my legs begin to feel like jelly. I can't take one more step. I take a seat on the hot, dry sand.

There are little shells in the soft sand. One of them is larger than the others. It is white with a peach-colored edge. I rub my finger on its outside surface, feeling roughness and bumps. Inside, the shell feels smooth and polished, like glass.

I hold onto it, making sure I do not let it go.

Looking out onto the water, I see a small boat. It is just a dot on the big ocean, but I can still see the motion of it going up and down.

The boat sails over a huge wave. The wave starts rushing toward me. I am paralyzed for a moment, frozen by how big it is. My body begins to relax when the wave gets smaller as it comes closer to the shore.

The sound of laughter grabs my attention away from the frightening waves. A brother and sister run by me. They cannot be older than ten.

The boy is chasing his sister like he is a cat and she is a mouse. He copies every turn or move she makes to stay right behind her.

Every few seconds, she looks back. She checks to see if he is still there. They are playing tag, a game almost every child loves to play. The girl runs toward the water, trying to make it harder for her brother to tag her. She laughs.

"What are you laughing at? I'm coming!" yells the boy.

The girl is wearing a striped, pink-and-white swimsuit. It has a flamingo in the middle, covered in purple and pink sparkles. Sand fills her short, brown hair, but she doesn't notice.
The boy has on a neon-green swim shirt with blue sleeves. They both smile. Their teeth are white, but gapped.

The boy's jog turns into a fast run, like he is in a track and field tournament. His legs and arms move together with every step.

"Ah, no!" yells the girl.

The boy tags her, but this does not frustrate the girl.

"Rematch?" she asks.

"Yes, let's do it! Go! Go!" the boy says excitedly.

They keep running, but in the opposite direction. There is a figure in the distance, but all I can see is a shadow.

"Guys, come here! Come on! It's time to eat!" the figure calls.

The boy grabs his sister's hand. They run toward the woman. Soon, they fall into the arms of their mother. She gives them both a kiss on the forehead.

The sky is pink and orange-red, like the sun. Over time, the sun gets low in the sky, saying goodnight to everyone.

Snap.

It all goes dark. Black.

"You're never here! I barely see you anymore!" my mom yells. The arguing was back.

Why can't I stay at that beach forever? After hearing the door slam, I run to the window. I look out to see who left.

Mom walks to Celeste's house with her head down and her eyes full of tears. As I watch Mom knock on her best friend's door, I hear my phone ringing.

It is probably Maya, calling about the party tonight.

We were close friends in middle school. But as soon as we went to high school, I let go of everyone I knew. I isolated myself, building a wall between my classmates and me. Maya has been trying to tear that wall down since freshman year.

The phone call is followed by a text message. I grab my phone from my bed and read the message from Maya.

Hi, Leila! We're all going to Grace's house to-night. I am hoping you can come. Just let me know!

I put the phone on my desk and walk to the opposite side of the room.

FIVE

The Big Easy

This morning is strange.

I cannot hear the usual sound of Dad's fork scratching against his plate while he eats breakfast.

I cannot hear Mom's favorite news channel playing on the television.

Are Mom and Dad not downstairs?

A single tear spills out of my left eye. I quickly wipe it away. I look calm, but my mind is tangled and messy. Pretending like everything is fine, I walk downstairs.

Mom is not sitting on the couch and listening to current events. Dad is not sitting at the table, looking at his phone while he eats the breakfast in front of him.

There is only one other place Mom can be: Celeste's house.

Still wearing my pajamas, I head to the home next door. As soon as I step outside, I begin to shiver. My arms and legs are covered in goose-bumps like a polka-dot dress.

Mom sits on the patio with a cup of coffee in her hand. She's talking to Celeste.

"Mom! Mom! Mom!" I yell.

"Leila, what's wrong?" she asks with a worried look on her face.

"Where is Dad? I can't find him anywhere," I say.

"Well, I don't know either," Mom says.

"Is he at work? Is he meeting up with a friend?" I ask.

Mom looks down. She avoids making eye contact with me. With her hands neatly folded in her lap, she says nothing.

She begins to speak, but quickly stops.

Right away, I knew.

"Mom, did Dad leave?" I ask, with a lump in my throat.

She keeps staring at the ground. She acts like I have not said anything.

I repeat myself. "Did Dad leave?"

Finally, she raises her head. She puts her coffee on the table beside her. She looks me in the eyes.

Slowly, she tells me what I wish was not true.

"Yes, but I'm sure he'll be back soon," she says.

"What do you mean, 'he'll be back soon?'" I ask.

"He left, but he'll be back," she says.

I shake my head. "I don't think he will be, Mom," I say.

I don't know what else to do, so I turn around and run back into my house. While running toward the stairs, I come to a sudden stop.

There it is. The cockie jar. It is still empty, with only crumbs and a few chocolate chips left.

As my lips quiver and my cheeks start to burn, I race to my room. There, I deal with this the only way I know how. I escape through my mind.

The poster with musical instruments grabs my attention as I take a step into the room.

I lay my head on the purple, fluffy pillow and rest on the bed. I close my eyes. As soon as I do, I am thrown into the other world.

Trumpets and saxophones are the only things I hear. A group of four men is playing at the end of the street. Their feet move to the beat they are playing. They tap along with the short and long notes. The group of people watching grows from five to fifteen in less than a minute. A woman behind me claps to the rhythm. Her young daughter, whose long hair is tied with a red ribbon, dances.

A black baseball hat is on the ground. It is filled with mostly one-dollar bills. I reach into the front pocket of my jeans. I pull out a five-dollar bill, tossing it onto the large pile of money.

My eyes follow their fingers sliding across their instruments.

Snap.

It all goes dark. Black.

I open my eyes to the same posters I closed them to.

How could Dad leave us? What did I do to deserve this? Why did I have to be born into this messed-up family?

These thoughts flood my mind like an overflowing river. I want them to disappear, right away.

I am pushed back into the scene.

Music.

Jazz.

A different place.

I wait for the song to end before leaving. The combination of all the brass instruments makes a beautiful song. The music finishes with the saxophone playing a high note. It is followed by loud clapping from everyone.

I walk across the street with a smile on my face. There is nothing more relaxing and calming than music. Music pulls me in, letting me forget about everything else happening in my life.

Music is a distraction. Sometimes, all I need to survive is a distraction.

Snap.

It all goes dark. Black.

Why do I keep opening my eyes? Why is this not working?

One more time. One more time. One more time.

I head down a busy alley, filled with dozens of restaurants. I can still hear the catchy jazz music.

Snap.

It all goes dark. Black.

Helplessly, I stand up and leave my room. For once, it did not work. I could not escape.

I expect Mom to still be at Celeste's house. I am surprised to see her in the kitchen.

She's looking out the window and drinking water. She plays and twirls with her silky, brown hair. She only does that when she is so overwhelmed that she does not know what else to do.

"Mom, are you okay?" I ask.

"Yes. Don't worry, Leila," she answers. She's still keeping her back toward me.

"Well, then, turn around," I say.

Tears run down her red cheeks like water droplets out of the sky. After brushing her hands over her face to wipe away her tears, she gives me a fake smile. As always, she is trying to protect me.

"Mom, you don't have to smile. I know how you're feeling. Don't hide it, please," I say.

She can't hold back her tears for a second longer. They begin to fall from her eyes.

I go to her quickly. I wrap my arms around her tightly, like a child hugs their favorite stuffed animal.

The only thought in my mind at this moment is escaping. I want to be walking down a deserted street. I want to be looking at beautiful landmarks. I want to be listening to wonderful music. Anywhere but here.

Maybe, just maybe...

The streets are filled with little cottage-like houses. Each house has a small lawn with the greenest grass I have ever seen.

Children play together outside their homes. Some of them throw a ball back and forth. Others sit criss-cross applesauce on their porches, chatting with each other.

I walk past a house with a sister and a brother eating red, crispy apples and peanut butter. They're having a picnic on a blanket on the grass. They chew silently while their eyes look around. They look at the big oak trees, blooming flowers, and dogs walking by with their owners.

There is hardly anything on the ground. It's like a big vacuum cleaned the whole town. Following the clean, concrete path, I reach a cute little restaurant. The menu is written on a chalkboard. It lists different kirds of burgers, hot dogs, fries, and sodas.

People are gathered inside the restaurant. More people are waiting in line outside. The customers talk to each other like best friends. It's like they have known each other for their whole lives.

I overhear two middle-aged women talking about the hot weather. They are both wearing flowered dresses.

A father and son talk about a school event that is later today.

Three teen g rls look at their phones. They all have their long, thick hair in high ponytails.

"I'll have two chili dogs, a medium ice water, and a large order of fries," says an older man inside the restaurant.

There are only two employees. One takes the customers' orders. The other makes the greasy, mouthwatering food.

Across the street are a handful of shops and stores. There is a shop with a couple of women standing outside, looking through the window. Their hairstyles are the same, like they both go to the same hairstylist: short, straight hair with bangs.

Next door, there is a gift shop that sells stuffed animals, coffee mugs, toys, t-shirts, and postcards. The cashier reads a fashion magazine. She skips the pages with lots of writing.

Two women behind me go into a nail salon. They go to the back of the room, where all the different nail polishes are displayed. The glass bottles are organized by their colors. The red polishes are lined up first and the purple polishes last, like a rainbow.

It seems like a perfect place to live. What could be wrong?

An ice cream shop attracts a crowd of people. A girl walks out with three scoops of mint chocolate chip ice cream in a sprinkle-covered waffle cone. Following her, a boy holds a sugar cone with one scoop of strawberry ice cream and one scoop of chocolate ice cream.

I stand at the end of the long line for what feels like forever. Finally, it is my turn to order.

"Can I please have two scoops of blueberry cheesecake?" I ask.

"Sure, miss. That'll be two dollars and eighty cents," the man behind the counter says.

After handing over the money, I walk to the back of the store. I wait for my ice cream.

In a few minutes, an employee calls out my order. I walk out of the shop with my favorite dessert.

As soon as I step outside of the air-conditioned shop, the hot, humid weather hits me.

I notice that the ice cream is already beginning to melt. I lick around the cone. My mouth moves from the top of the ice cream to the edge of the cone.

The ice cream is rich, creamy, and a bit tangy. Chunks of graham crackers hide inside the vanilla and blueberry ice cream. I pick them up with the end of my tongue. I suck on them until they are as flat as a pancake before swallowing.

Even though it has only been twenty minutes, it feels like I have seen everything in the town. There is nowhere else to go. I went into most of the shops and walked by all the restaurants. But there is still one popular street I have not gone to: Peach Street.

People love walking down this street because of its tree canopy. The tall trees block the sun from the street, making a perfect shade.

A woman is working in her garden. The plants, flowers, and fruit trees are a pretty sight for the rest of the street. The red, pink, yellow, and green colors stand out.

As I walk by, she waves and smiles at me. I do the same. She is talking with her friend, who is sitting on the porch and drinking lemonade.

Snap.

It all stays the same.

I am in Smallview. It's the town I have grown up in and will keep living in until I graduate from high school.

Mom and Celeste are together, as usual. But Dad is not around.

I'm tired from walking all over town. I sit on my house's dry, dead grass. It feels like sandpaper against my bare legs, but I stop thinking about the discomfort. There is so much more to think about.

Smallview is not like New York, Paris, Las Vegas, Malibu, or New Orleans, but I am here. I cannot escape.

My daydream escapes are not the answer. They are a break from Smallview, but they are only temporary, short-lived. Dreams will never solve the problems in my life that I am using them to escape.

Maybe I should stay in the present. Maybe I should stop hiding away from Maya and other friends. Maybe I should have faith that my dreams will come true someday, because I have control over them.

Maybe I should stop thinking about the future when the present is so precious.

But, after all, maybe all of this will happen. I cannot make any promises.

Maybe, just maybe.

About the Author

Sophene Avedissian is a passionate writer. She is a contributor to Youth Civics Initiative, GEN-Z NE, and The Teen Magazine. Additionally, she serves as the Social Issues Platform Lead of the organization INK-Spire and serves as a Senior Editor for Polyphony Lit.

About the Publisher

Storyshares is a publisher focused on supporting the millions of teens and adults who struggle with reading by creating a new shelf in the library specifically for them. The ever-growing collection features content that is compelling and culturally relevant for teens and adults, yet still readable at a range of lower reading levels.

Storyshares generates content by engaging deeply with writers, bringing together a community to create this new kind of book. With more intriguing and approachable stories to choose from, the teens and adults who have fallen behind are improving their skills and beginning to discover the joy of reading.
For more information, visit storyshares.org.

Easy to Read. Hard to Put Down.

www.ingramcontent.com/pod-product-compliance
Lightning Source LLC
Chambersburg PA
CBHW072234190626
46809CB00017B/1976